William B. Eerdmans Publishing Company
Grand Rapids, Michigan

ANTOINE

© Copyright 1986 by Scandinavia
Publishing House, Nørregade 32, DK-1165 Copenhagen K.
English language edition first published 1987
through special arrangement with Scandinavia
by W. B. Eerdmans Publishing Co.,
255 Jefferson Ave. S.E. Grand Rapids, Michigan 49503

Printed in Singapore

ISBN 0-8028-5022-7

ANTOINE
and the Magic Coin

Doug Sewell

Have you ever not seen something but felt its presence? That was how it was when I arrived one December night in Antoine's village.

Though hidden in darkness, mountains enveloped me. I felt their breath.

Early the next morning I was awakened by Antoine jumping on my bed. He had so many stories to tell about the mountains, I could not retell them all to you.

But what enthralled me most was how God came alive for him in the mountains - a God of majesty, yet also of tenderness. I came to admire the respect the people of Antoine's village held for the mountains and how it showed in the way they honoured each other. And how like the crew of the Air Glacier helicopter rescue team, they also risked their lives

'For the LORD is the great God....in His hands are the depths of the earth and the mountain peaks belong to Him'

(Psalm 95)

**William B. Eerdmans Publishing Company
Grand Rapids, Michigan**

Antoine was a dreamer. He often dreamt of exploring high mountains and hidden valleys. What he did not know was that someday his dreams would lead him and his best friend, Wilhelm, into the most dangerous adventure of their lives.

The old Swiss village where Antoine lived was surrounded by mountains. Antoine enjoyed them best in winter when they were covered with fresh powder snow. Then he could sled all the way to school.

For most of the year, the mountain slopes were covered with flowers and lush green grass. Milking cows grazed high up on the slopes. Each cow wore a different sounding bell so she could be recognized by her owner farmers. Before the winter's snow fell the cows were brought into big barns stocked with hay.

Antoine's village looked much the same as it used to hundreds of years ago. The large wooden houses, called **châlets**, all faced south to catch the sun. The church bells rang from the top of the hill every hour, echoing between the mountains.

The people in Antoine's village spoke French. In another valley close by, they spoke German. A third language, Italian, was spoken in yet another part of Switzerland. This was a country of mountain peaks, sparkling lakes, pretty alpine villages and ancient castles.

Castles! One thing Antoine often dreamt of discovering was a castle he could call his own. He had been searching for over a year. And at last the day came when Antoine believed his search was over.

One frosty autumn day Antoine was exploring a mountain creek where he had heard there had once been a castle. As he climbed the rocky slope, he was lost in daydreams about far off times when the legendary Wilhelm Tell, with a crossbow and arrow, had set the Swiss free from a wicked ruler.

Suddenly, Antoine noticed something caught between two rocks. He looked at it closely. It was a very old, bronze coin, unlike any other coin he had ever seen. One side was worn smooth. The other side revealed the faint image of a square cross. The coin felt icy cold. Antoine breathed on it so the bronze surface sparkled.

"Is it a magic coin?" he wondered. "Won't Wilhelm be excited! I'll show it to him at school tomorrow." Antoine and Wilhelm were closest friends. They did almost everything together and shared all their secrets with each other.

On the way home Antoine imagined he was a Swiss soldier who had won the coin in battle. Long ago Switzerland was made up of many smaller principalities that often fought against each other. Then they had needed fortresses and large castles to protect themselves against attack.

Antoine knew there had not been war in Switzerland for hundreds of years. Switzerland had become a symbol of peace because it was a country that did not take sides in war. But Antoine could not keep his thoughts from wandering back to the past, which seemed so much more exciting to him.

The next morning Antoine arrived early at his village school. Some of his classmates were playing on an icy hill, getting their pants soaking wet. Antoine looked for Wilhelm, but he was not there. Wilhelm had to come a long way by bus and was often late. Antoine clutched the coin in his pocket. He was not going to tell anyone except Wilhelm about the coin. The bell rang just as Wilhelm arrived. As the class marched inside, Antoine stepped back along the line until he was next to his friend.

"I have found a magic coin!" exclaimed Antoine softly. He slipped the coin into Wilhelm's hand.

"It sure looks old," said Wilhelm, keeping one eye on the coin and his other eye on where he was going.

"Yes, I think it's a wishing coin," Antoine whispered as they sat down at their desk.

"A wishing coin!" Wilhelm closed his eyes and squeezed the coin tightly. "I wish for a castle. And I will be the prince!" Wilhelm shared his friend's love of castles. He opened his eyes.

"I'm going to save my wish," Antoine told him. "Maybe I'll need it more some other time."

At that moment the teacher leaned over Wilhelm's shoulder and asked to see the coin. "Where did you boys get this?" she asked, turning it over in her hand.

"I found it at the bottom of a creek bed. I think it's very old," answered Antoine.

The teacher nodded. "It's difficult to say just how old it is. It might date from the time of the counts of Gruyère. They ruled this valley over four hundred years ago."

"Did they have a castle?" asked Wilhelm.

"They had several," replied the teacher. "The largest is still standing at Gruyère, but most are just ruins overgrown by the forest."

When the teacher left, Antoine's eyes were sparkling. "Let's try to find one of those castles. Maybe we can find other old coins or weapons!" he challenged Wilhelm.

"**Why** not come and visit me at the same time?" Wilhelm suggested. "There are some old ruins in the forest we can explore. And my grandfather can even show you how he makes cheese."

"Great!" replied Antoine.

So one weekend just before Christmas, Antoine packed his backpack and travelled by bus to the farm where Wilhelm lived with his grandfather. In a beautiful narrow valley, the old farmhouse was snuggled in a blanket of snow, and long icicles hung from the edges of the roof. Wilhelm and his grandfather were waiting at the end of the road to meet Antoine. Their friendly faces warmed him after the long journey.

Once he was settled, they took Antoine to the cheese-making shed. Wilhelm's grandfather began to stir a copper vat filled with milk. All thoughts of coins and castles faded as Antoine watched. He had never seen milk become cheese before.

"How does it become hard?" he asked.

"I add something called 'rennet' to the heated milk. Rennet makes it curdle and go thick," explained Wilhelm's grandfather. "I separate the lumpy parts called 'curd,' from the liquid using a cloth filter. Then I pour the lumpy part into a mold to set."

"Cheese fondue is my favorite food!" Antoine boasted.

"Yes, Swiss cheese fondue is famous all over the world. Gruyère cheese makes a delicious fondue," declared the old man, stirring the milk a little faster.

"Gruyère! The counts of Gruyère!" shouted Wilhelm, remembering again the reason for inviting Antoine. "We're going to look for one of their castles!"

"You be careful if you go into the forest," warned grandfather. "I'm too old to come looking for you if anything should happen."

"We'll be careful, Grandpa!" said Wilhelm. Wilhelm knew roaming in the mountains could be dangerous. His own mother and father had been killed in an avalanche, or mountain snowslide, many years before. But Wilhelm's desire for an adventure with Antoine was stronger than any fear.

The next morning at the earliest sign of light, Antoine and Wilhelm packed a breakfast of cheese and hard rolls and set off into the forest. Wilhelm's German shepherd, Ruedo, led the way.

They climbed into the mountains for several hours until the valley lay far below. Another thick layer of snow had fallen during the night. Occasionally a branch loaded with snow collapsed, and a flurry of white would scurry down the slope.

"Remember, we must be careful not to start an avalanche," Wilhelm warned. "They can start very easily in fresh snow like this."

The boys climbed until they reached a clearing where several stacks of logs were piled up beside each other. "This wood must be for the new châlets," said Antoine. "There's no one around. Let's climb to the top of that pile of logs to get a better view of the valley."

But the logs were covered with snow and were slippery. When Antoine stepped on the top log it wobbled, rocking backwards and forwards. Antoine became scared. But Wilhelm, still at the bottom and unaware of his friend's predicament, began to laugh. Ruedo sensed the danger though, and started barking. But it was too late.

Suddenly, the top log jerked, and the whole pile groaned. "Watch out Wilhelm! The logs are...!" screamed Antoine. Then he jumped and landed safely in a pile of soft branches.

Wilhelm saw the logs rolling towards him. He turned and ran down the steep slope, slipping and falling. A terrible grinding, crunching noise followed him. But Wilhelm could not move quickly enough. One of the rolling logs smashed into a small tree, sending it toppling over.

Wilhelm was crushed beneath the fallen tree.

Antoine crawled down the slope to where Wilhelm lay trapped. One of Wilhelm's legs was crushed beneath the tree, and a branch had fallen onto his head. Blood was running from his mouth.

"Wilhelm can you move?" shouted Antoine. But Wilhelm lay motionless. Antoine began to tremble with fear. He tried to lift the tree off Wilhelm's leg, but it was much too heavy.

Ruedo licked Wilhelm's face and whimpered as he lay by his side.

"What are we going to do?" Antoine asked desperately.

The dog barked as if to answer.

"Go home and get help!" cried Antoine, not even sure anymore of which direction Wilhelm's house was. He could not know but Ruedo was actually trained as an avalanche dog. Ruedo stood a moment and whimpered again. Then he ran off down the mountain-side, sure of his way.

Once again Antoine tried his hardest to move the tree. It would not budge. Antoine felt his heart pounding inside his head. "God, please help Wilhelm!" he prayed.

He heard no sound except for the mild winter breeze whispering through the trees. He sat for a long time thinking about what he should do. He wondered what Wilhelm's grandfather would think when Ruedo came home alone. Grandfather was too old to come looking for them, or to help.

Antoine began to cry. He wished he had never heard of the Gruyères or their castles. He wished he had never found that old coin. He wiped the dirt and blood off Wilhelm's face. "Please stay alive Wilhelm. God, please help Wilhelm stay alive!" he sobbed.

Several hours passed. Antoine sat huddled against Wilhelm, trying to keep him warm, when he heard a motor sound overhead, way above the tree tops. Running out from under the trees, he saw a helicopter circling high above.

Antoine waved his cap, and the helicopter circled once more, lowered, then landed in the clearing. Ruedo jumped out of the helicopter followed by two men. They ran down to the place where Wilhelm lay.

"What happened?" shouted the men. Antoine could hardly hear their voices over the roaring engines.

"He was knocked down by the logs!" Antoine yelled back. "A tree fell on him!"

The men bent over Wilhelm, who lay still and lifeless. Their faces were pale and grave.

"No!" cried Antoine. "No! He can't be dead!"

The men shook their heads. Then they covered Wilhelm with a blanket and wound a bandage around his head. They tried to move the tree, but it was too heavy.

The pilot ran back to the helicopter and took off. Hovering overhead, he lowered a cable to be tied around the tree. Then, ever so slowly, the helicopter lifted the tree trunk. At the same time the other man carefully pulled Wilhelm free.

They strapped Wilhelm's legs together and laid him on a stretcher which was lifted into the helicopter. The rotor blades whirred loudly overhead, kicking up leaves and sawdust.

The pilot shouted to Antoine, "We'll fly straight to the hospital! You come with us! The dog can find his own way home."

Aboard the helicopter, Antoine was fastened into the back seat. Wilhelm lay in a special bunk. The engines roared to full power and the ground dropped away. Suddenly, the helicopter tilted at an angle and swung sideways. It raced off across the tree tops.

Antoine saw his own village appear below. People ran out of the châlets to look up. Then the rooftop of the hospital came into view. As the helicopter landed, a cloud of snow lifted off the ground. Before Antoine had realized it, Wilhelm was taken from the helicopter and carried away.

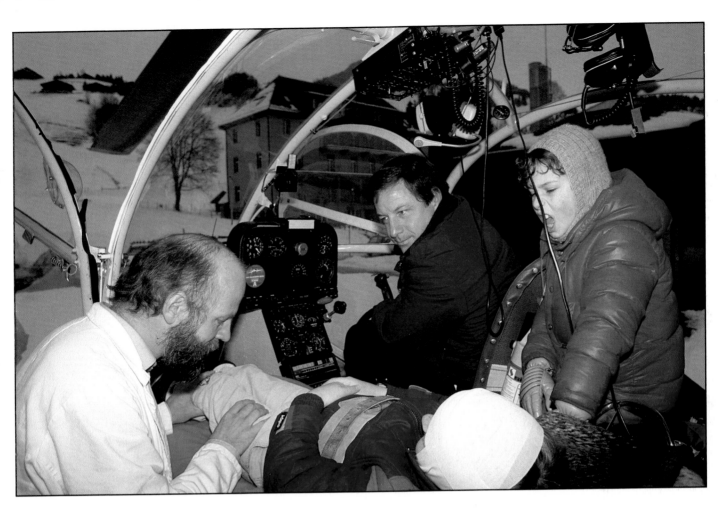

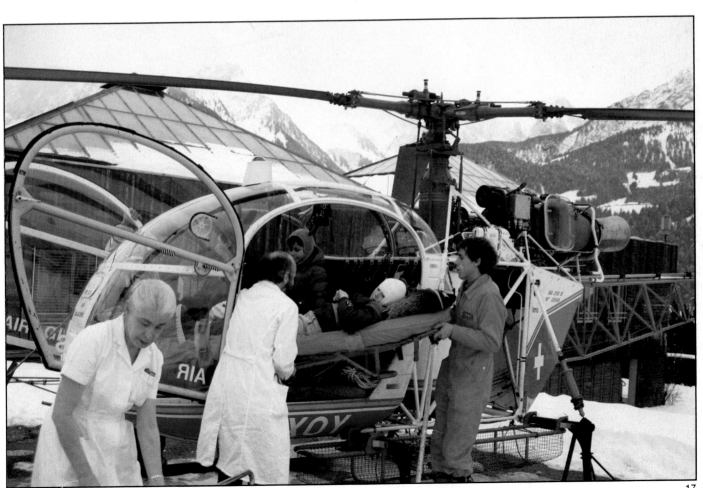

Many days passed. Antoine had
returned home to celebrate Christmas with
his own family. On Christmas eve another
layer of fluffy snow fell from the skies.

Some of the village children, wrapped in
thick coats and with their hands tucked into
mittens, were out on the narrow streets
singing Christmas carols. An old man was
selling roasted **maroni**, a type of chestnut
cooked in a pan over a coal fire. Colored
lights twinkled in snow-laden trees in the
village square.

Antoine gazed gloomily out of his iced-up
window. His mother and father tried to
cheer him up. But Antoine was not feeling
any Christmas spirit at all.

"I'm scared," he admitted. "Wilhelm has
been unconscious for more than a week.
What if he never wakes up?"

"We're all afraid, Antoine," replied his
father. "Wilhelm is in good hands at the
hospital. But we all must go on praying for
God to heal him."

"Poor Wilhelm. It's all my fault. I got him
excited about finding a castle. I started the
log rolling. I was so dumb! Poor Wilhelm!"
cried Antoine.

"Antoine, you must not blame yourself,"
answered his father. "You can only learn
from it and allow God to forgive you. And
be sure to forgive yourself. We all must
experience things that are difficult to
accept. That's how we grow up."

"If only there were something I could do to
help Wilhelm."

"You can pray. Ask God to give you an
idea that would help him."

"But God doesn't answer my prayers,"
said Antoine. "In the forest when the tree
fell on Wilhelm, I prayed so hard. But God
didn't say anything."

Antoine's father put his arm around him. "I
believe God did answer your prayer," he
said. "Didn't the helicopter find you? And
you were not hurt. You were there for
Wilhelm. And you can go on praying for
him."

About that time the bells of the village church began to ring, calling people to the Christmas eve service. Village churches all over Switzerland were ringing their bells then. Antoine could hear some of them echoing through the valleys.

Antoine's family climbed the steep hill behind their châlet. On the way, they met other people from the village.

The old church was almost full when the family arrived. The wooden balcony which had the best view was almost bursting with people. Antoine's family found a seat off to the side.

Everyone whispered excitedly. Soon it became very warm inside. Those still wearing coats started to take them off. Antoine noticed that some of his classmates were dressed in costumes from different parts of the world. They were going to perform a pantomime. This Christmas eve service was about all people from every country celebrating Jesus' birth together. A large Christmas tree with candles waiting to be lit stood at the front.

Antoine thought about how much Wilhelm would have loved to be there with them. A tear glistened in his eye. He missed Wilhelm so much.

When everyone sang the first carol Antoine felt a big lump stick in his throat. All the same, the bellowing organ made a joyful noise.

The lights were turned off and one by one the candles on the tree were lit. Slowly, the whole church filled with a glimmering light which made everyone's faces glow.

Antoine felt a flicker of hope. Perhaps God would help Wilhelm, he thought. Wouldn't that be wonderful? Then it really would be a joyful Christmas after all.

When the time came for the people to leave the church and go home, each took a little candle with him. Antoine carried two, one for himself and the other for his best friend.

Once back home in their cosy châlet, Antoine's father gathered his family around him. "Before going to bed," he said, "we're going to pray for Wilhelm."

Mother stoked up the wood fire and heated some milk for chocolate. She reached for a big copper kettle that stood in the corner. The floorboards creaked as she walked on them. There was a lovely woody smell in the châlet and the low ceiling made it feel very cosy.

The family sat around the kitchen table lit by a lantern. Father opened the family Bible and read about a man whose little daughter was dying. Jesus had said to the man, "Don't be afraid; just believe, and she will be healed." And Jesus had gone to the little girl's house. Though all the neighbors had thought she was already dead, Jesus had held the sick girl's hand until she woke up.

"If we pray for Wilhelm will Jesus heal him?" asked Antoine's little sister, Michelle.

Her mother answered, "We know Jesus loves Wilhelm and will not leave him alone."

While they prayed, Antoine imagined Wilhelm alone in his hospital bed. He knew the doctors and nurses often stood around Wilhelm's bed talking about what they could do to help him. But they had done all they could. For them there was nothing to do but wait.

"Dear Jesus," Antoine prayed, "please make Wilhelm well again. You love him. Your love can heal. I know it can."

Suddenly, Antoine looked up and blurted out, "I know! I know what I can do!"

The others stared at him. "What? What?" they asked at once.

"It's a surprise!" beamed Antoine. "I'm not going to tell you until tomorrow."

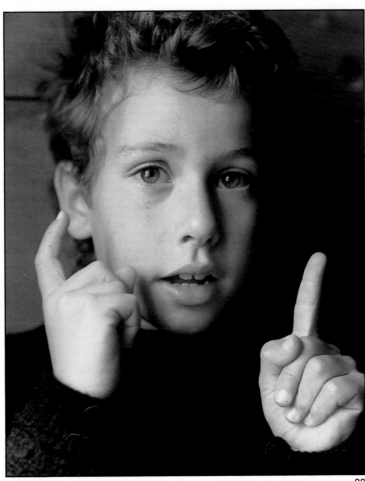

Early Christmas morning when Antoine's parents came downstairs they found his little sisters playing by the Christmas tree. The family had exchanged presents on Christmas eve. Overnight a few more gifts had turned up which had hung in stockings around the bottom of the tree. They now lay scattered all over the floor.

"Where is Antoine?" asked Mother, looking around the room. "Is he still asleep?"

"No, he's in his bedroom and won't let us in. He's been awake in there for hours," Michelle answered.

Antoine's mother went upstairs and knocked on his door. "Antoine, are you all right?" she asked.

Antoine's voice came through the door. "Yes Mom, but please don't come in! I'll come downstairs soon."

Not long after, Antoine marched downstairs, proudly carrying a lovely cardboard castle he had built himself. Held together with glue and bits of tape, the castle had a drawbridge and several towers. Its walls were decorated with stars, a crescent moon and other patterns making it very colorful.

"What is this Antoine?" asked his father.

"Is that my Christmas present?" chirped Michelle as she clapped her hands and hopped up and down.

"I'm going to give it to Wilhelm," replied Antoine. "When he had only one wish to make, he wished for a castle!"

Michelle's face dropped. "But Antoine, Wilhelm won't be able to see it. He won't even know you are there or that it is Christmas!"

"I think he will," declared Antoine. "I think God will help him feel how much I care about him, enough to build him a castle and make him feel like a prince on Christmas day."

"Okay, Antoine. I can see this means a lot to you," interrupted Father. "I'll drive you to the hospital. I just know it will mean a lot to Wilhelm too!"

Antoine wrapped up the castle. He was so excited about seeing Wilhelm, his hands were shaking as he cut the wrapping paper.

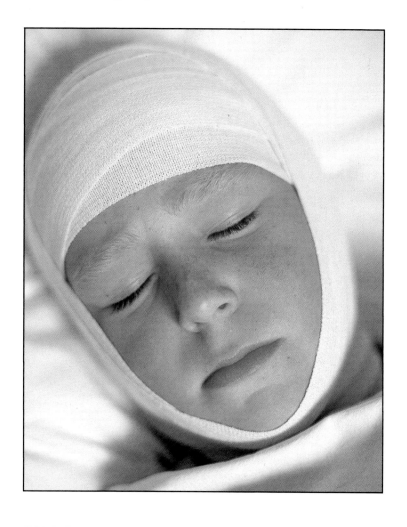

In the waiting room at the hospital Wilhelm's doctor spoke to Antoine and his father, "Wilhelm is still a very sick boy. But since it is Christmas day, you can see him for a moment."

A nurse opened the door to Wilhelm's room. Antoine took a deep breath as he went in with his sisters. "Hi Wilhelm," he whispered. "I've brought you a Christmas present and...." Antoine stopped when he saw Wilhelm's eyes stayed closed and his face unmoving. "And we prayed for you last night," he continued.

"I'm afraid he can't hear you, he's unconscious," whispered the nurse.

Antoine gently grabbed Wilhelm's arm and squeezed it. "Wilhelm! I've made you a castle!" he spouted out.

When Antoine said the word "castle," Wilhelm eyelids fluttered for just a second. Antoine jumped back in surprise.

The nurse was excited. "Keep talking to him! I'll call the doctor!" she exclaimed.

Antoine didn't know what to say next. Finally he cried, "Wilhelm! Wilhelm! God loves you and so do I. It's Christmas and I just know you're going to get better because we've all been praying for you. And I've made you a great big castle!"

Antoine unwrapped the paper and opened the box. He lifted the handmade castle out and displayed it on the bed before Wilhelm. Wilhelm opened his eyes slowly. "Cas-tle?" he mumbled.

Wilhelm was so weak. He could not remember what had happened to him in the mountains, but he recognized Antoine and his eyes were open for the first time in many, many days. As he struggled to keep them open he repeated, "Cas-tle?"

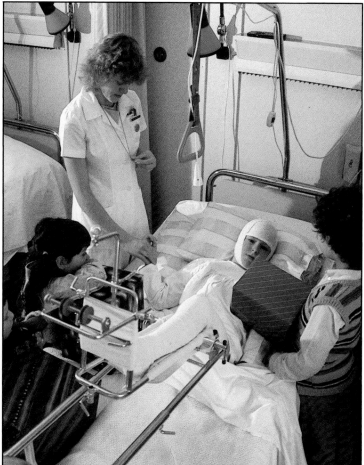

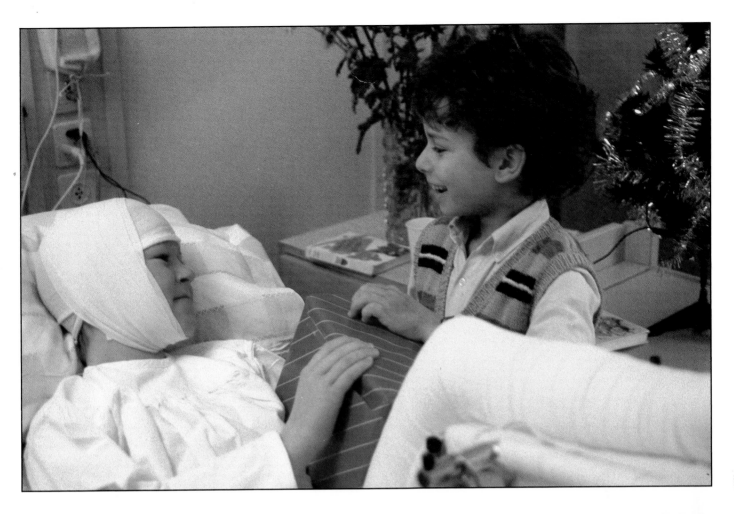

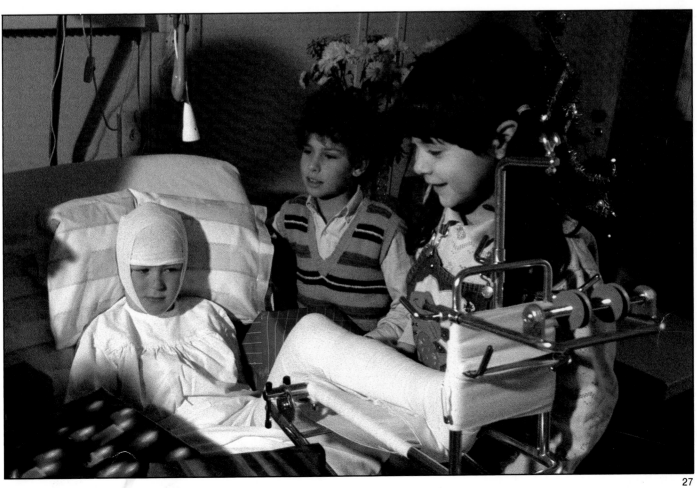

Wilhelm recovered more and more each day. Several weeks later, his broken leg looked somewhat better and he was pronounced well enough to leave the hospital. He was almost sad about leaving, however. Two of the nurses had become his special friends.

Since Wilhelm still needed some extra care, Antoine's family invited him and his grandfather to live with them for a while. One day, on the balcony of the châlet, Antoine showed Wilhelm his magic coin again.

"Remember this coin? It has brought us nothing but bad luck, Wilhelm," he said. "For the last weeks, I've felt guilty and sorry. I knew it was my fault you got hurt. But I felt so helpless. I couldn't do anything except pray. But I sure did that. Oh, I prayed so hard."

"Didn't you wish on the coin for me to get well, Antoine?" asked Wilhelm.

"No, this coin won't help anybody. God's the One who healed you."

"It was the castle you made me that helped, Antoine!"

"Well, maybe it was. But it was God's love that made me want to do something for you. What really matters is trusting Him and caring for others."

Wilhelm took the coin and looked across the valley. "Antoine, even if I were the prince of a castle, I wouldn't be as happy as I am now. Because we are best friends."

Antoine put his arm around Wilhelm's shoulder. "I'm glad we didn't find a castle," he said. "Princes always used to fight against each other. If we were both princes we wouldn't be able to be best friends."

"I'm glad, too. Though I must admit, I would have let you win," Wilhelm said with a grin.

The boys burst out laughing at the thought of that.

Antoine and Wilhelm never did lose their desire for adventure. Skiing across the mountains one day, they stopped at the top of a steep slope. Antoine pulled the old Gruyère coin out of his pocket. "See Wilhelm," he shouted, "here it goes!" Antoine threw the coin as far as he could. The boys watched it whizz through the air, gleaming in the sunlight. It landed far down the slope and sank into the deep, soft snow.

"But Antoine!" exclaimed Wilhelm. "You could have sold that coin or given it to a museum!"

"Nope. That coin belongs to the mountains. Maybe another boy, hundreds of years from now will find it again. And maybe the coin will in some way help him to trust in God."

"Hurrah for the mountains and for the One who made them!" shouted Wilhelm.

And the two boys skied off down the slope.